KIRK SCROGGS

SNOOP TROOP

ATTACK OF THE NINJA POTATO CLONES

L B

Little, Brown and Company

New York Boston

Little, Brown and Company

Hachette Book Group
1290 Avenue of the Americas, New York, NY 10104
Visit our website at lb-kids.com

Little, Brown and Company is a division of Hachette Book Group, Inc.
The Little, Brown name and logo are trademarks of Hachette Book Group, Inc.

The publisher is not responsible for websites (or their content)
that are not owned by the publisher.

First Edition: April 2015

Library of Congress Cataloging-in-Publication Data

Scroggs, Kirk.
Attack of the ninja potato clones / Kirk Scroggs.—First edition.
pages cm.—(Snoop Troop ; 2)
Summary: "In this early chapter book/graphic novel mash-up, fifth grade private eyes Logan and Gustavo use their doodling and detective skills to solve the mystery of a tiny ninja who is stealing their town's supply of potatoes. Over a dozen pages of bonus backmatter are loaded with extra puzzles and doodle activities!" —Provided by publisher.
ISBN 978-0-316-24277-6 (hardback)—ISBN 978-0-316-24275-2 (ebook)—ISBN 978-0-316-36454-6 (library edition ebook) [1. Mystery and detective stories. 2. Stealing—Fiction. 3. Potatoes—Fiction. 4. Cloning--Fiction. 5. Humorous stories.] I. Title.
PZ7.S436726At 2015
[Fic]—dc23
2014043207

10 9 8 7 6 5 4 3 2

RRD-C

Printed in the United States of America

Special thanks to Steve Deline; Joanna Stampfel-Volpe;
Jaida Temperly; Danielle Barthel; Hiland Hall; Mark
Mayes; Joe Kocian; Mamacita; Corey; Candace; Charlotte;
and Isaac; and a mega macho mustachioed thanks to
Andrea Spooner, Deirdre Jones, Tracy Shaw,
Russell Busse, and the rest of the Little, Brown Troopers!

An Important Message from the Narrator

Hey, amateur private eyes!

Some spud brain is stealing all of Murkee City's potato supply. French fries, Tater Tots, yams, you name it! Pretty soon we'll all be eating crayons and glue if this keeps up! See if you can help the Snoop Troop crack the case by paying close attention, especially anytime you see a magnifying glass like the one right here. Now, if I can only find my car keys, I can get out of this creepy alley! This narrating is dangerous work!

CHAPTER 1
HOT POTATO

A lazy, peaceful afternoon on Bakersville Lane . . .

Birds are chirping. . . .

Butterflies are fluttering. . . .

Old Man Jorgensen is watering his petunias. . . .

Old Man Jorgensen's dog is watering Old Man Jorgensen. . . .

All is tranquil with the world.

Until the silence is broken by wild, piercing shrieks coming from an abandoned ice-cream truck!

Is it an elderly woman being kidnapped? A baby screaming for its pacifier? A cat with its tail caught in an electric egg beater?

Ah yes, I forgot. It's fifth-grade powerhouse private eyes Logan Lang and Gustavo Muchomacho. Ever since they started the Snoop Troop Detective Agency in Logan's mom's old ice-cream truck, they've been sharing trade secrets with each other.

5

Well, at least it looks like you two have become best friends.

"Best friends" might be stretching it a little.

Good buddies?

Nope.

Two humans who barely tolerate each other?

We're more like water and dirt. Together we make mud.

Yeah, or oil and vinegar. Together we make salad dressing!

All of a sudden, a million emergency vehicles zoom by with sirens wailing!

Wheelie is Logan's cranky old dog. Ever since he was a puppy, he's been known to eat a variety of things he isn't supposed to . . .

Like Logan's mom's wedding cake . . .

Uncle Fred's wooden leg . . .

And let's not forget the Cinco de Mayo Jalapeño Incident of 2012.

Luckily, this isn't the first time Wheelie has snarfed the remote, and Logan knows just what to do.

CHAPTER 2
AISLE OF TERROR

The Almost Fresh Grocery Store. When Logan and Gustavo arrive, the joint is crawling with cops and killer bargains. I mean, just look at that sale sign. Organic buttermilk for $2.99 a carton? They charge twice that over at Partial Foods on Main Stree—

Shhhh! Hold it down, narrator dude. I know you're excited by good deals on dairy, but we don't want to get spotted by the police.

Sorry, I got carried away. Just how do you expect to sneak past the police anyway?

Uh-oh.

It looks like Gustavo has slipped into the store unnoticed. That's Captain Mosely of the Murkee City Police Department and his deputies surveying the crime scene. The joint is a topsy-turvy wreck.

Logan sneaks in like a stealthy panther and joins Gustavo in a barrel of roasted peanuts. She's a little upset with him for sneaking off. He is technically still in training.

19

Look! Captain Mosely's interviewing Mr. Mister, the grocer. We need to move in closer so we can hear what they're saying.

I've got just the thing!

My spritzing Old Man Mustache. With this gray facial fur, this apron, and my swollen nose, we can slip right past the po-po.

NEW FROM SWISS UPPER LIP

YOUR MUSTACHE AUTHORITY

OLD MAN MUSTACHE

WITH SPRITZING ACTION!

FEATURES TWO 10-OZ SPRAY NOZZLES.

ORDER NOW AND GET A FREE OLD MAN HANDKERCHIEF!

HONK!

KEEPS UPPER LIP HYDRATED AND SHINY.

HANDY FOR GARDENING.

SPRAY BUTTER ON FOOD WITH EASE!

POP CORN

ARTIFICIAL BUTTER CARTRIDGE SOLD SEPARATELY.

Moments later, a kindly old grocer steps onto the scene spritzing the produce.

22

Pay attention to Mr. Mister's description and draw the suspect on a piece of scratch paper, the chalkboard, or your best friend's forehead while he's napping!

Captain Mosely sees right through their disguise and rips off the grocer's apron.

While Captain Moseley is yelling . . . er, giving his skilled team of experts a pep talk, Logan and Gustavo set out to search for more evidence.

Au contraire! If you hadn't been napping when I showed you episode ten of the *Dame Edith Mysteries*...

...you would have noticed she used dried coffee grounds to reveal wet footprints in the rose garden.

The grounds clump up on anything wet.

Now we just follow the trail of prints!

Wow! The janitor is going to hate your guts!

31

The footprints lead to the aisle of frozen foods, a cold and lonely place.

Logan senses someone lurking amid the TV
dinners and frozen lima beans.

Suddenly, a bite-sized ninja bursts out of the pizza section and hurls a frozen Sausage and Mushroom Supreme!

BONK!

The whirling disc of death with extra garlic smacks Logan in the noggin!

Ow! Who knew a frozen pizza could be so painful?

It says right here on the box: "Made with sharp cheese."

The peewee punk pounces into the Meat Department and leaps up onto a table . . . then makes his escape through an air vent in the ceiling!

Mr. Mister, an amateur potato expert, confirms Logan's theory. It is indeed a toe-shaped potato—or a pota*toe*, one might say. Logan and Gustavo share their discovery with Captain Mosely.

In case you hadn't noticed, Logan really likes
Tater Tots.

CHAPTER 3
THE MURKEE TALENT POOL

Murkee Elementary School. It's the next morning, and the hallways are abuzz with gossip about the Great Potato Robbery. Principal Shrub tries to ease everyone's minds about the tater shortage.

To make matters even tenser, it's the day of the big Mini Murkee Talent Show. After lunch the kindergartners are set to wow the entire student body with an explosion of raw talent and cuteness.

Never resting for a second, Logan brings her notes and sketches on the potato theft to the auditorium. She is joined by an unexpected guest.

Something about that pale blond munchkin looks awfully familiar.

Uh-oh.

49

Moments later, the Snoop Troop find themselves waiting outside Principal Shrub's office.

Shrub calls them in for a stern talking to.

Principal Shrub lets them off with just five detentions, with time off for good behavior.

CHAPTER 4
A SECOND HELPING

After school, Logan feels pretty rotten watching Gustavo clean out his desk. It doesn't help that he's making his sad puppy-dog face.

Suddenly, there's a breaking news flash on the TV!

Actual surveillance photo from Suds & Spuds!

BAKED POTATO

PLAIN SPUD... $2.99	DRY CLEANING
ADD ONS	PANTS ... $5.99
CHEESE ... $.99	DRESS SHIRT... $3.99
CHILI ... $.99	SUIT ... $20.00
CHIVES ... $.99	SUPER HERO CAPE...$10.00
HOT FUDGE ... $.99	

WE PRESS PANTS AND PANINIS.

CASH ONLY

SODA

$2.99

LAUNDRY

PANTS

TATERS

POTATO BAR

SUDS

Look closely!

CLUE

SUPPORTING PUBLIC TELEVISION

MYSTERY

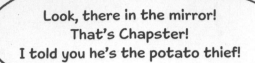

Suddenly there's a knock at the door!

Logan slowly opens the door to find . . .

AAAAHH!

Greetings, Snoop Troopsters. I bring an offering of homemade Gouda cheese.

It's Chapster!

Gee, uh, thanks. Why are you here exactly?

Just to say there are no hard feelings and that my pediatrician, Dr. Snote, said I have no broken bones from being so brutally tackled.

That's nice. Hey, as long as you're here, maybe you could tell us if you've ever been to the Almost Fresh Grocery Store or the Suds & Spuds?

Never to the Suds & Spuds, but I always go to the grocery store for free watermelon samples. So juicy. So delicious.

As he leaves, Chapster makes one last kind and incredibly spooky offer. . . .

> If you need me, I live just across the street in the dilapidated manor. Just wave. I'll be the one in the window, watching your every move. Ta-ta.

Once the little creep...er, uh, tyke is gone, Logan gets an idea. She pulls a novel called *Sherlock Holmes and the Crumpet Thief* from her huge mystery library.

In the book, Sherlock Holmes sets a trap for the suspect on page seventy-two. He puts out a plate of crumpets and waits.

I get it! We can do the same thing with some spuds!

But I thought you had given me the boot?

You're on probation. If you haven't tackled any more kindergartners by the end of this case, you're back on the force.

Deal!

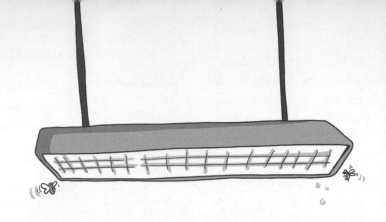

CHAPTER 5
OPERATION SMACKDOWN

The next morning, the Murkee Elementary office is hustling and bustling with the usual bunch of teachers, office ladies, and barfy kids looking to see the school nurse.

Miss Macky, an office lady, guards the intercom microphone with a yardstick. Only she can make announcements without approval from Principal Shrub or, if he's unavailable, the president of the United States.

Office lady yardstick fighting stances

Fortunately, Logan has the perfect plan and Gustavo has the perfect mustache for getting the job done.

While Miss Macky shows Gustavo to the copy room, Logan darts for the intercom and puts on her best old-lady voice. . . .

It doesn't take long for Miss Macky to figure out she's been duped.

Luckily, Logan and Gustavo give her the slip without suffering the sting of the yardstick.

CHAPTER 6
A CLEAN FIGHT

Five minutes later. The janitor's closet. A lone bag of spuds sits on an overturned mop bucket. Logan and Gustavo wait in the shadows for the potato thief to take the bait. . . .

Nothing seems to be happening. Are you two sure this plan is going to work?

Suddenly, the little nightmare ninja gives Gustavo a swift kick in the chops!

Then he swoops in for the spuds, but Logan lays down a slick pool of pink bathroom soap!

Logan ties up the little rascal and Gustavo tears off the ninja suit to reveal . . .

It's crazy! The broom closet is full of Chapsters!

Suddenly, a Chapster swoops in with a blinding window-cleaner face-spray attack while another Chapster smacks Logan with a broom!

Then, a different Chapster unleashes the electric floor waxer on Gustavo!

Argh! The agony...oh, wait. This actually feels pretty good. Would you mind doing my lower back? Oh yeah. That's the spot!

Logan delivers a blistering karate chop, and her hand slices right through Chapster's fingers, sending tiny, crisp fingerling potatoes into the air!

The Chap attack is unrelenting! But Gustavo seems unfazed.

Finally, the Chapsters all escape through the air vent with the taters!

Logan and Gustavo run out of the broom closet and burst into Miss Perkle's kindergarten class next door!

Moments later, in the principal's office yet again, Shrub has a few words to yell about Logan and Gustavo's behavior. . . .

Shrub gives them five more detentions and sends them on their way.

CHAPTER 7

BRINGING HOME THE BEACON

After school, the Snoop Troop combs the neighborhood, waiting for Gustavo's homing beacon to beep when they get close to the potato sack.

SNIFF!
SNIFF.

TOXIC WASTE

3+ NOT FOR CHILDREN UNDER THREE

All of a sudden, Gustavo's mustache goes off like an alarm clock gone haywire!

The bushy beacon has led them to a crumbling, rusty, old garden shed. It looks about as inviting as a rattlesnake cupcake party.

Inside, it's dusty and junky and smells like sawdust.

There are books strewn about everywhere. And we're not talkin' just any ol' books—these are books about potatoes!

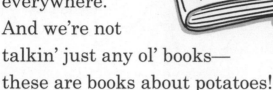

On the ground sits the sack full of socks and dirt. The little mini-mustache beacon is beeping away.

See if you can uncover the secret message in this pictogram!

Suddenly, they catch a whiff of something cooking, accompanied by strange munching and crunching sounds.

On the other side of the door sit a whole table of Chapsters! They are smacking and chomping and using their greasy little hands to stuff their mouths full of potatoes!

As they munch on the potato products, a TV in the corner features a live report from Dr. Snote about the toe-shaped potato. A shadowy figure emerges from behind some crates! That's when all the Chapsters suddenly notice Logan and Gustavo!

The Chapsters have spotted you. I suggest you guys get the heck out of there!

Gustavo trips on a rock on the way out and grabs on to a tarp. . . .

Behind the tarp is a giant tank with a Chapster suspended in it. From his shoulder sprouts a tiny disgusting mini-Chapster!!!

CHAPTER 8
HEY, BUD!

Within twenty minutes, Logan and Gustavo have called the cops and the shed is surrounded by Captain Mosely and his men.

All right, you in the shed! Come on out with your hands up and your potatoes where I can see 'em!

Mosely decides to force his way in!

99

Someone must have covered up his or her tracks. The shed is clean, and Captain Mosely seems none too pleased to have been called out on his night off.

Back at the ice-cream truck, Logan and Gustavo dine on Fudgysickles and review what they've learned so far. . . .

It's obvious that if this mystery is going to be solved, we're gonna have to do it ourselves. Take a look at this.

Logan points at a scientific potato book she checked out from the Murkee Elementary library.

Logan starts doodling on her dry-erase board. Soon she arrives at her theory, and it's a doozy. . . .

Logan also concludes that the shady figure they saw hiding in the shadows in the shed is the same person who cloned Chapster.

I think we get your point! So, let me get this straight: The suspect is someone who has access to Chapster's DNA?

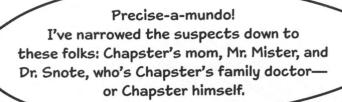

Precise-a-mundo! I've narrowed the suspects down to these folks: Chapster's mom, Mr. Mister, and Dr. Snote, who's Chapster's family doctor— or Chapster himself.

CHAPSTER

CHAPSTER'S MOM

DR. SNOTE

MR. MISTER

Our next question is figuring out where the army of Chapsters plans to strike tomorrow. Somewhere that has a large supply of gold.

Logan lays out a map and searches for the most likely location for a gold robbery.

It doesn't take long to pinpoint the locale.

CHAPTER 9
THE UNUSUAL SUSPECTS

It's the next day. Friday. 3:30 PM. As soon as school lets out, Logan and Gustavo rush over to the Almost Fresh Grocery Store. All is normal. Patrons are shopping. Sales are brisk. Diapers are half off.

In the examining room, Logan and Gustavo ask Dr. Snote whether or not he's ever gotten a DNA sample from Chapster.

There's not much more the doc can tell them, so they bid him farewell.

And question suspects they will. Next stop on the list—the lair of Chapster!

Okay, if there's one place less inviting than that shed full of clones or Dr. Snote's office, it's Chapster's house. Even a ghost might think twice before visiting this joint!

Inside, Chapster and his mom are busy drawing portraits of one of their prized stray cats.

After Logan politely refuses the fungi refreshments, she asks Chapster and his mom what they know about DNA, clones, and growing potatoes.

Gustavo slaps on his
NosePix 500 printer-beard
accessory and prints out
all the photos he took
of the suspects.

Logan examines the photos.

Wheelie examines his butt.

With only thirty minutes to go before the great gold robbery, Logan makes a special announcement.

An Important Message from the Narrator

Hey, all you super sleuths! Here's your last chance to figure out who cloned Chapster before the Snoop Troop reveals it in the next chapter. If you can't figure it out, go back and look at each page with a magnifying glass labeled "Suspect" or "Clue," like the ones right here. Come on—impress me!

Which one of these shady characters clones kids, swipes spuds, and is gunnin' for gold?

 **CHAPSTER'S MOM?** She likes martial arts and sure could use the money from a gold robbery for a home makeover.

 **MR. MISTER?** He knows his taters.

 **DR. SNOTE?** He's a smart doc with access to DNA.

 **CHAPSTER?** Maybe he cloned himself. He likes to grow weird things in dark places.

Turn the page to find out who's a slimeball super villain!

CHAPTER 10
WHO LET THE SPUDS OUT?

Logan and Gustavo gather everyone in the living room to reveal the perpetrator's identity.

Ladies and gentlemen, dogs, cats, creepy cheese-and-fungus experts—we are about to unearth the identity of the criminal scoundrel. Then I'd like to follow it up with a song. Something jazzy that we can all dance to.

127

So, if Chapster and his mom and Dr. Snote are all innocent, who does that leave?

Suddenly, Mr. Mister bursts in with his posse of Chapster clones!

The clones tie everyone up in the living room. Logan asks Mr. Mister why on Earth he chose Chapster to model his army of robbing replicants after.

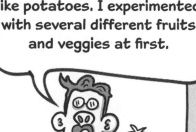

My Chapster clones are composed of potatoes, feed on potatoes, and reproduce like potatoes. I experimented with several different fruits and veggies at first.

The Bananachapster just did not work out at all. Very mushy and un-a-peeling!

Blarb! Blug!

Now I'm off to steal some gold! Don't even think about trying to wriggle free or call the cops, or the real Chapster gets it!

You brute!

After Mr. Mister leaves, Logan and Gustavo try to squirm free of the ropes. Unfortunately, they're so tight, even Wheelie can't gnaw on them.

133

CHAPTER 11
THE BIG CHAPSTACULAR!

Fort Bling Bling. 5:00 PM. It's quiet. Too quiet. Logan and Gustavo and Wheelie arrive on the scene ready to bust Mr. Mister and his Chapster crew.

Logan tries to warn the head of security, but he's not having it.

The clones have infiltrated the building! Everything gold is in danger!

Logan and Gustavo are overtaken by the pernicious pipsqueaks.

How in the heck are you guys going to get him down?

Gustavo's Grappling Stache V-7 launches a hook that latches on to the basket. Logan slowly shimmies up the rope attached to it.

She makes her way into the basket and boots out any unwanted passengers.

Scanning the horizon, Logan looks for any spot from which Mr. Mister could be controlling his army of spuds.

Suddenly, the Chapster clones start jamming together into a huge mega clone clump that keeps getting bigger and bigger!

The clones have formed into a behemoth Chapsterzilla!

Logan, it looks like you're gonna have to stop Mr. Mister! Gustavo's too busy trying not to get stomped into mulch!

You're right! Chapster, it's time we put our playground swinging skills to good use!

Word!

They start swinging the basket to and fro until the contraption can't possibly swing any higher!

Madame, is this a bad time to inform you that I am easily prone to motion sickness?

At the highest point of the swing, Logan disconnects the basket, and they go hurtling through the air like a rocket!

The grocer's truck is flattened. His satellite dish destroyed!

Unfortunately, even with the satellite dish destroyed, the mega Chapster is still going strong, packing up all the loot and laying waste to the city!

Gustavo's words suddenly awaken something in Logan, and for once it's not anger.

The humongous Chapster freezes in place at the last second!

Finally, the air is filled with the sounds of sirens and screeching tires as Captain Mosely pulls up with his men.

CHAPTER 12
BACK ON THE FORCE

Days later, the Snoop Troop decides to take it easy. Chillin' and relaxin' are all that are on the agenda.

After all, it's exhausting being heroes. For saving the city, they had been awarded the Golden Scalloped Potato medallion. . . .

The clones had their mind-controlling potato chips snipped, and formed the world's biggest boy band. They are known for their killer mash-ups.

And Wheelie finally returned the remote control. . . .
Please don't ask how.

But Logan and Gustavo's day of relaxation is interrupted by an unexpected guest. . . .

Our private eyes cherish the remainder of this peaceful day because they know it will not last.

There is already a foul wind and strange smell in the air. . . . Trouble is on the way!

DOODLE SNOOPS

CLASSIFIED

**Warning:
The following secret files
may require doodling,
scribbling, heavy thinking,
and, possibly, yodeling!**

Oh, and if this book doesn't belong to you, don't draw in it or Miss Macky might get smacky!

Attention, shoppers!

Captain Mosely needs your help!

HOW TO DRAW CHAPSTER

1. Start with his stylish hairdo, like half a grapefruit turned over.

2. Add his beady little eyes, like two black-eyed peas.

3. Don't forget a sniffer and his two front teeth.

4. Check out the set of ears on this kid!

I shall bring you homemade cheddar every day!

5. How about some stubby little arms? Careful—those hands are coated in bologna grease!

6. Be sure to add his favorite T-shirt! Now you have a new best friend!

Visit lb-kids.com to print out these activities.

HOW TO DRAW A POTATO

First draw an oblong blob, like a football that's been left in the sun all summer.

2. Now add little bumps and eyes.

This tater's getting ripe, so let's add a little sprout coming out of it, like a stylish ponytail.

4. Slap some leaves on there!

Now add some more eyes. We're talking real eyes this time, with luscious lashes!

6. Add some teeth and a swanky sweater. Congratulations! Your date for the Murkee Elementary Dance has arrived!

HOW TO DRAW A NINJA

1. The eyes come first, angry and round, like enraged kumquats.

2. Next is the nose, like a lounging lima bean.

3. Then draw a square around it, like a party envelope. This is the mask of the ninja.

4. The shape of the head must match he who wears the mask.

5. Now, draw the body, preferably in a martial arts battle stance!

6. Finally, add classic ninja weaponry, like the throwing star and salami nunchacku!

Hiiiii YAH

Visit lb-kids.com to print out these activities.

HOW TO DRAW
CAPTAIN MOSELY

Draw the eyes with furry-caterpillar brows above them.

2.
Now, a big ol' schnozz with an impressive mustache, like two big, fuzzy tarantula legs.

Time for the square jaw and round ears.

4.
Follow that with a big, round head of hair, like a poodle that's just stepped out of a dryer.

Make sure you draw his body in a stance that says, "Don't mess with me, kid!"

6.
Finally, give him a tie and don't forget the sassy one-liner.

I'm gettin' too old for this.

CRACKPOT

A security cam snapped two pics of the Snoop Troop in action, but something doesn't look right about that second photo.

Visit lb-kids.com to print out this activity.

SNAPSHOT

Pick out the differences before it gets plastered all over the news. Answers are on the next page. No cheating, or Chapster will force you to eat his homemade cheese-curd porridge!

Help! Mr. Mister, the mean green grocer, has sent another pictogram! See if you can figure it out before that scoundrel strikes again!

(answers on next page)

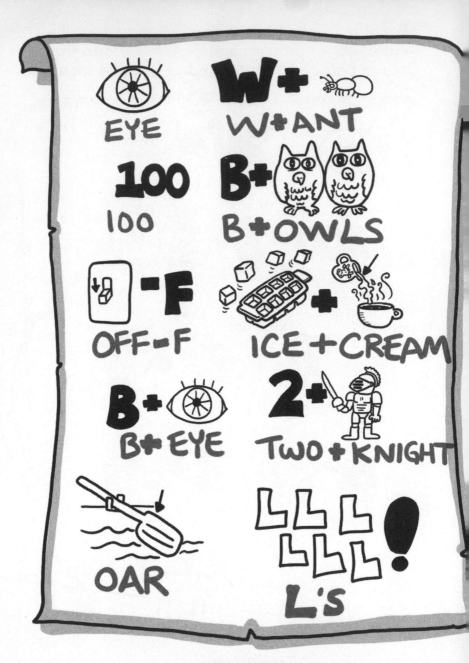

Answer:
I want 100 bowls of ice cream
by tonight or else!

WHAT'S UNDER LOGAN'S MAGNIFYING GLASS?

Sketch the magnified clue!

- It is green and slimy.
- It has bulging eyes.
- It has a really long tongue.
- It has webbed toes and fingers.
- It is eating a juicy house-fly quesadilla.

Visit lb-kids.com to print out this activity.

Something snuck into the bakery last night and squeezed all the fresh bread! Help us catch this hooligan by sketching the suspect before it makes off with any more muffins!

- It had big eyes.
- It had a long tongue that was split at the end.
- It was fifteen feet long.
- It didn't have arms or legs.
- It was wearing a lovely bow on its head.

Visit lb-kids.com to print out this activity.

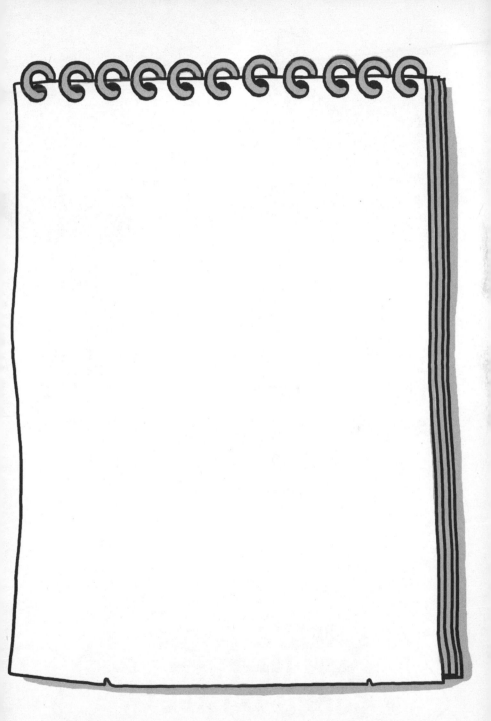

WORD SEARCH

```
Z  G  M  I  C  R  O  S  C  O  P  E  I  O  A  C  K
C  O  J  C  A  T  S  V  H  H  N  I  N  J  A  S  I
H  U  X  O  L  H  M  C  A  T  K  T  A  I  L  W  D
I  D  S  O  B  P  N  F  I  E  C  R  O  U  C  I  S
P  A  R  M  E  S  A  N  R  S  H  A  K  D  H  S  C
K  I  T  T  Y  P  E  T  B  T  E  P  F  C  C  S  L
Q  U  E  S  O  S  L  A  A  T  D  A  T  A  R  X  O
S  T  I  N  K  Y  S  D  L  U  D  H  R  P  F  E  N
C  A  T  N  I  P  W  B  L  B  A  F  J  S  T  S  E
D  N  A  Q  O  F  O  L  A  E  R  D  T  W  I  N  S
```

Look for words involving the three C's: Cats, Clones, and Cheese!

Visit lb-kids.com to
print out these activities.

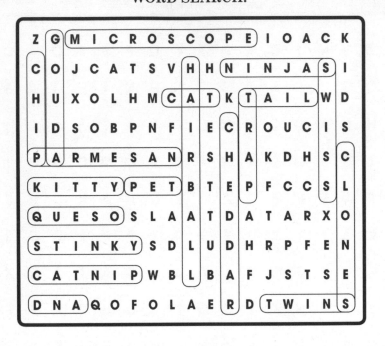

KIRK SCROGGS

is the author and illustrator of *Snoop Troop: It Came from Beneath the Playground*, as well as the Tales of a Sixth-Grade Muppet series and the Wiley & Grampa's Creature Features series. He lives in Los Angeles.